Spring Has Sprung!

by Kiki Thorpe
illustrated by Tom Brannon

Simon Spotlight

Based on the TV series *Bear in the Big Blue House*™
created by Mitchell Kriegman. Produced by
The Jim Henson Company for Disney Channel.

 SIMON SPOTLIGHT
An imprint of Simon & Schuster Children's Publishing Division
1230 Avenue of the Americas
New York, New York 10020
Manufactured in The United States of America
First Edition   10 9 8 7 6 5 4 3 2 1
ISBN: 0-689-83064-5

One bright morning, Bear poked his head out the door of the Big Blue House and took a sniff. "What's that smell?" he asked himself. He sniffed again. "I smell sunshine and fresh dirt and grass just starting to grow. Why, it's you! You smell like spring! And spring means it's time to plant things around the Big Blue House."

Bear got out his gardening tools and was just about to plant the first seeds when Pip and Pop came out the door.

"Where are you two going?" Bear asked the otters.

"To the otter pond!" said Pip.

"To ice-skate," added Pop.

"We love ice-skating!" Pip and Pop shouted together.

Bear looked around the yard. The snow had almost completely melted in the warm sunshine. "Uh, guys," Bear started to say, "maybe today isn't the best day for ice-skating . . ."

But the otters were already running down the path to the otter pond.

When Pip and Pop got to the pond, they found a surprise—the ice was gone! The otters couldn't believe their eyes. Just days before, the pond had been frozen and slippery. Now it was murky, muddy, and wet.

"Someone has stolen all the ice," Pip said in dismay.

"We'd better tell Bear," Pop said.

"Bear! Bear!" the otters cried, running back to the Big Blue House, "All the ice from the pond is missing!"

"That's what I was trying to tell you before," Bear said. "Spring is here. When spring comes it gets warmer, and all the snow and ice melts."

"You mean no more sledding or snow angels?" Pip asked.

"No more snow forts or skiing or . . . *or ice-skating*?" Pop cried.

"Nope, not until next winter when it gets cold again," Bear told them.

"Next winter!" Pip gasped. "But Bear, next winter is a long, long time away."

"Woe is me." Pop sighed. "What will we do now?"

"Guys, there are lots of great things to do in the spring," Bear said. "Why right now I was just about to—"

Before Bear could say anything more, Ojo came running up.

"Bear!" she shouted. "Pip and Pop! Come see what I found!"

Bear, Pip, and Pop followed Ojo to a small patch of snow. There, right in the middle of the snow, was a beautiful purple flower.

"Isn't it cool?" Ojo asked, pointing at the flower.

"Yeah, cool," Pip and Pop agreed. "Where did it come from?"

"That's another thing that happens in the spring," Bear told them. "Flowers and other plants start to grow. In fact, I was just about to plant some flowers in my—"

Suddenly they heard a noise overhead—"Wheeeeeeee!"

"Hey!" said Bear, "that sounds like . . ."

"Treelo! What's up, Treelo?" Bear asked.

"Treelo up, Bear," Treelo said. "Treelo up in trees. Treelo find surprise."

"A surprise?" asked Bear. "Let's go see what it is."

"We love surprises!" Pip and Pop shouted.

"Look!" Treelo said to his friends.

Pip, Pop, and Ojo all looked into the tree branches and saw a nest full of eggs. Suddenly—*Crick! Crack!*—one of the eggs cracked open, and a tiny baby bird came out.

"Oooh," said Pip, Pop, Ojo, and Treelo all at once.

"That's another thing that happens in the spring,"
Bear said. "All sorts of baby animals are born. Come on,
guys. Let's leave this little bird alone so he can get used
to his new home."

"Wow!" said Pip. "There sure is a lot of stuff going on in the spring."

"Yeah," Pop agreed, "even if there was ice on the otter pond, I'm not sure we'd have time to go ice-skating after all."

"Spring is a great time of year," Bear said. "And one of my favorite things to do in the spring is to plant—"

"Bear!" This time it was Tutter shouting. "Bear, look what I just got in the mail!" Tutter was waving a small package at his friends.

"What is it, Tutter?" Bear asked.

"It's a shovel, Bear, a shovel for a mouse! My Grandma Flutter sent it to me. I'm going to use it to plant seeds in my garden."

"Funny you should say that, Tutter, because planting seeds is exactly what I was about to do. Why don't you all come help me?" Bear said.

Bear's friends all agreed that gardening would be the perfect way to spend a sunny spring day. Bear found shovels and gloves and packets of seeds for everyone to use. They spent the morning digging and planting and watering the seeds. Everyone was having a great time, when suddenly . . .

Treelo jumped into a tree and started swinging happily from a branch!

"Whoopeeeee!" he shouted.

"Hey, Treelo!" Bear said. "Are you okay?"

"Treelo great, Bear," Treelo answered. "Treelo happy!"

"Hmm. This looks like a case of spring fever," Bear said.

"You mean Treelo's sick?" Ojo asked.

"No, no, Ojo." Bear said. "Spring fever is just being excited about spring. Sometimes all the sunshine and green grass and good smells make you feel like jumping and singing. In fact, I'm getting the itching and scratching to do a little dancing myself."

With that, Bear started doing the cha-cha-cha right there in the dirt. When Bear starts cha-cha-cha-ing it's hard not to follow. Pretty soon Ojo, Treelo, Pip, Pop, and Tutter were all dancing, too.

"Blue sky!" shouted Treelo.

"Butterflies!" Ojo cried.

"Hey, look!" Tutter said as he did the limbo under a tulip leaf. "More flowers!"

"I love sunshine and flowers," Pip said as he shimmied to the left.

"I love baby birds and planting seeds," Pop said as he hopped to the right.

"You know what?" both otters shouted together. "We love spring!"